# The Adventures of Mister

by

S.D. Holmes

AuthorHouse™
1663 Liberty Drive, Suite 200
Bloomington, IN 47403
www.authorhouse.com
Phone: 1-800-839-8640



First published by AuthorHouse 1/7/2009
ISBN: 978-1-4389-3786-1 (sc)



Printed in the United States of America
Bloomington, Indiana

This book is printed on acid-free paper.

# Finding a Home

This looks like a nice sunny spot. I think I'll just lie here for a short nap. Perhaps when I wake up, it will be time to eat. This is a great place to live. Say, where are my manners? My name is Mister, and I would like to tell you about my life and how I came to be where I am.

It all started a few short years ago. I was just settling in with my original keepers (they were never family) when I had to go to the doctor for a checkup. He checked me over from head to rear paws and even took my temperature (rectally, need I say more?). A couple days later, my keepers received a phone call, and before I could say "cat nip," I was outside looking in. At first I thought it was a mistake, but as I continued to try and get back in the house, they kept kicking me out. Finally, after finding me hiding in the basement, they put me in the car, and we drove off. Now, I don't like the car, so I kept howling. The female keeper reached back and pounded on my carrier to make me be quiet. It really gave me a start. After what seemed like an eternity, the car stopped. I was very relieved because I needed to use the box.

My carrier was lifted out of the car, and with the door opened, it was tilted so I would slide out. I crept out slowly and at first acted very cool. I stretched and looked around, expecting to see the house, but soon realized nothing looked familiar. I thought we all might just be stretching our legs, when all of a sudden, the door to the carrier was slammed shut, and I was on the outside. Although I don't usually like it, I tried to get back in. Instead of opening the door, a hand reached down and pushed me away, hard. I headed for the car, but this time was kicked in my side. I was stunned and short of breath. As my head began to clear, I heard the car door close and the car drive off.

I sat in silence, too shocked to even lick my wounds and wondered what to do next. It was getting dark; I was hungry, and I was lost. I started to walk along the road but soon realized how dangerous this could be.

I got off the road and began to walk on the grass. As I walked across one yard, a dog started barking and I quickened my pace. With my stomach growling, I headed for some tall grass to look for some tuna or catnip. All I could find was a mouse. I think it wanted to play because it started to run. I was too tired to play, so I pounced on it and chomped down on its neck. It wasn't much, but at least it was something. I curled up in the tall grass feeling sorry for myself and finally fell asleep.

I don't know when I've spent a more restless night, but it was soon morning, and the sun was shining. I decided to move on and find better accommodations. The next few days were more of the same. I got pretty good at finding food, but it just wasn't enough.

I finally stumbled upon a neighborhood with lots of bushes to hide in. I knew I needed to be very careful and observe things for a few days. I figured I could watch by day and hunt by night.

I picked out a house that had some nice, full bushes in the front and decided to park myself there to keep an eye on things. The bushes would not only shield me from the elements, but also from the street. I could watch the entire world without being detected (or so I thought). I began observing a man who frequently came and went from his house. He seemed pretty happy-go-lucky and warranted a closer look. I moved in to observe him more directly. He pulled the car into the garage, and I was by the front door. Perfect! He disappeared in the house so I decided to rest.

I was in the middle of a nice nap, when these strange people woke me up. My first instinct was to run for it, but I decided to see how this was going to play out instead. The next thing I knew, there were people staring down at me, including the man I had been watching. He came out of the house and started to talk to me. It was different from any other time I had been talked to; it was in a calm and low tone. He came around the back of the bushes and began to stroke me while talking softly. I was still a little leery because of how those last humans had treated me. It felt good to be petted again, but I knew I had to wait to see how it would go. He went back in the house, and I took a nap. I had no idea (because I was out getting food) that the man came out later to check on me.

The next day was warm and sunny. I enjoyed the space in the bushes where I was hidden, but able to see what was going on. I was just beginning to doze off when a car pulled in the driveway and a woman got out. Oh no, she was coming toward me! I should run, but wait, she too is talking softly to me. She sat down on the front step and continued to try and coax me out of my spot. I held my ground, and soon the man was standing close by. I was so busy watching the woman, I never noticed him pull in. That's not good; I must watch more closely. The man came to me and started to pet me again. I was just starting to purr when I heard the woman say, "He looks hungry. Why don't you give him some food?" Next thing I knew, I was eating something very tasty. Food I didn't have to hunt for. Cool!

The people left, and I returned to my spot in the bushes. A short time later, I was awakened by voices again, only this time they were off in the distance. I thought I should check it out to see if I had any competition. I walked around the side of the house and heard the voices getting louder. I realized they were coming from inside a fenced in area, but quickly decided this was no problem since I could jump a fence.

Hey, it was the man and woman from the house, and to my surprise, chicks! Not only did really kind humans live here, but there were a couple of babes basking in the sun. I had started to walk with my best swagger toward the ladies, when I suddenly caught a whiff of something so appealing, I forgot what I was doing. I thought I had smelled something like it before, but it had been so long now since my first humans got lost, I couldn't really remember.

The man started petting me and playing rough. I really enjoy playing rough, and right then, I realized how much I had missed it. The woman was just watching, and the other ladies were totally ignoring me. I was having too much fun to stop at that moment and focused all my attention on the man.

When he finally stopped, I decided to go and check out the girls. Boy, were they stuck up. All I wanted was a little sniff; they didn't have to be so prissy. Oh well, the humans seemed glad to see me. I decided these were the humans for me. The plan was clear. I was going to be so cute, they would never want to see me go.

# MovingIn

Well, it was all working according to plan. Every evening I would greet my humans when they got home. I would act really cute in the backyard during their evening ritual back there. My man would rough me up and then rub my belly. He knew all the right spots to make me purr. Of course, I especially liked the scratching of my butt.

My humans really seemed to like me. My only problems through all of this were the girls. The gray one was OK most of the time, but the other one was a tough nut to crack. Every time I got near her, she would hiss and walk away. Reminded me of my first female human.

After a couple of weeks of this, the human woman told my man they should fix me a bed in the garage and put down some food and water. Although I continued to lick myself as if I didn't care, my heart began to race. I was so happy, I could have licked her on the lips!

My man disappeared for a short time, but returned with a big box. They cut the box down some to make it easier for me to get in to. I jumped a fence that was four feet high to get to them in the backyard, and they are cutting down a twenty-inch box. Humans!

I was carried to the garage and shown my new home (for now). There was food, water on the floor, and a blanket in the box. The bed was up on a shelf, which was really nice, but I much preferred the hood of the car. After a few days of looking pitiful, curled up in a ball on the car, they finally moved the box. Since they were so nice to me, I was very careful not to scratch the paint. I could really have done a number on it if I had wanted.

I was now in a very happy and peaceful position. I had a nice bed, water, and crunchy food. Life was good. I continued to explore at night and check out the surrounding area as well as catch on occasional tasty morsel. These humans had been so nice to me, I wanted to do something nice for them. I, of course, did the best thing I could for them and left a plump little mouse by the door. That is when the tone of the human woman began to change. Instead of thanking me for my great gift, she sounded, well, testy. In a somewhat controlled but louder voice, she told my man she did not want dead animals on the doorstep. If the mouse upset her that much, the rabbit by the backdoor would really raise her hackles. I decided to get the rabbit and hide it for a snack later.

My man seemed to like my presents and tried to explain it was a sign of affection. We were all in the backyard preparing for some barbecue chicken when, all of a sudden, my woman pointed a finger at me. This was not a playful gesture, but one of anger. She was upset because I was still trying to warm up to the girls and because of the mouse. I ran from her, and my man called me to him. See if I waste another snack on her!

# Getting a New Name

Several different names had been tossed around. Moses, because I was found in the bushes (yeah, right). Romeo was mentioned because I took off every night and crawled home early in the morning. A final choice was Mister because, well I really don't know why. I refused to even give Moses a second thought. I briefly considered Romeo because I did fancy myself somewhat of a ladies' man, but dismissed that as well. I liked Mister and that's what was picked.

Since I moved into the garage, my humans were nice enough to leave the door up a little, so I could come and go as I pleased. There was some discussion about something called a "doggie" door. I didn't know what it was, but with a name like that, it couldn't be good. My man just kept the door up and ignored the other discussion—that is—until that fateful night in September.

I had just left my bed to go use the facilities, when I heard my man raise his voice in surprise. As he yelled, I also heard the house door slam shut. When I finished what I was doing, I headed back to the garage. As I turned the corner, I saw this funny looking black and white cat come out of my area, probably eating my food.

I walked toward him, ready to give him a piece of my mind, when I caught a whiff. Obviously he had not had time to bathe because boy, did he stink! I decided to let him go, but if he ever came back, he was really going to hear it. Funny part about the whole thing, a couple of days later, the "doggie thingy" was installed. My garage door was lowered all the way, and my routine lifestyle was once again upset. Did I also mention the woman looked very smug throughout all this?

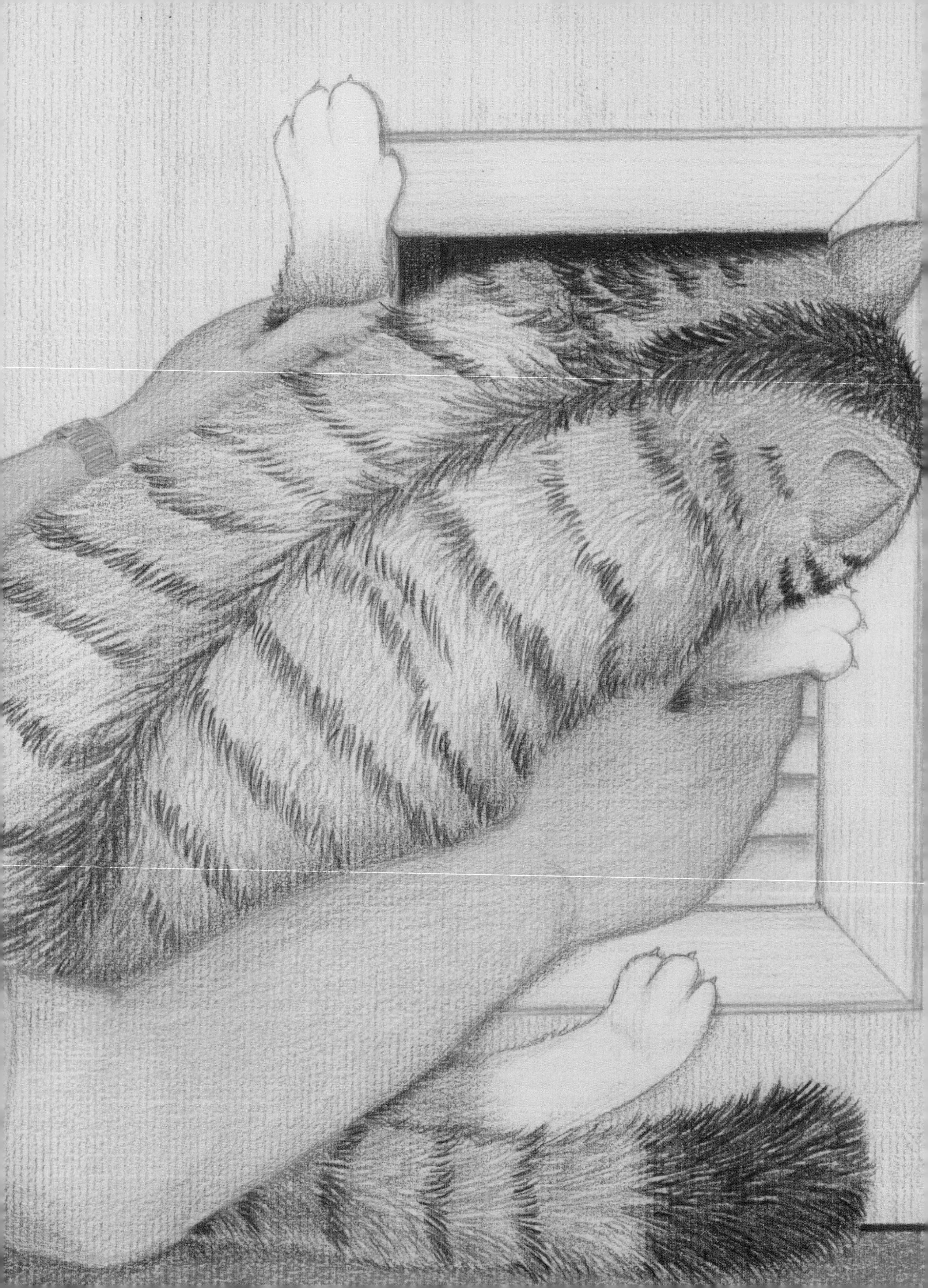

# The Doggie Door

Now, I was inside the garage with no way out, and I knew this couldn't be good. The cars had been moved out of the way. The house door was closed, and there was a human on each side of this mini-door. The woman grabbed me and began to shove me through this window looking thing. I thought she was trying to kill me. I firmly planted all of my paws along each side of this contraption and pushed back. I proved to be stronger than her because she fell down, at which point I took off. Being a garage, there was lots of stuff to run around, knock down, and hide under. I jumped onto a shelf, knocking things off in my path with the woman in hot pursuit, screaming for me to stop. Apparently she knew nothing about cats. We do NOT respond well (or at all) to commands.

My man, of course, thought all this was pretty funny, which seemed to infuriate the woman even more. She stomped out of the garage and into the house. Finally, I thought I could relax and come off the shelf. Boy was I wrong. He grabbed me and headed for the tiny door. The difference now was that the outside door was closed, and he was between freedom and me. He opened the flap to show me it was safe, and I remembered thinking, "If it is so safe, you try it." He began to push me through the door, and I decided to let him this time.

The really weird thing about all this was once he got me on the outside he wanted me to go back through to the inside again. He continued to shove my head through the door several more times. I saw no point to this exercise and let him know in no uncertain terms. By the time he was ready to stop, his arms looked like he had been berry picking.

That night, after dinner on the back patio, my man and I walked around the block for our evening constitutional. When we arrived back at the house, we went in through the garage, and he lowered the door—all the way! I was trapped. How would I get out? What if I needed to use the potty? I could get even for all I had been put through that day and use the first box I could find, but that wouldn't be smart. My man said goodnight and walked in the house. I was all by myself.

I decided to curl up in my box and sleep on it. As a cat, I like to sleep on everything. Since I do not own a watch I had no idea how much time had passed when I began to feel the urge. I looked at the closed door again and wondered what to do. I finally could wait no longer and approached the small door cautiously. I carefully placed a paw on the door and almost fell through it. It swung back and caught me in the head. I looked around to make sure no one was looking and remembered I was alone. I had to get outside, now, and decided to give this door a try. I crept up on it and placed my head against the panel. I pushed lightly and it opened. I stepped over the threshold with my front paws and was free, half of me anyway. I wiggled the rest of my body through the door and realized I was outside. I was so proud of myself, I was going to try it again when I remembered why I wanted outside in the first place. I was going on patrol; the door would be there in the morning.

I wanted to get back before my humans left for the day to make them think I suffered through a long night by myself. Unfortunately, I got hung up with the cutie down the street and was late getting home. The gig was up, and from that day on, the only way for me to go in and out was through the doggie door. For the record, I still think it is a stupid name.

# Bad News

The humans started wearing heavier outer garments because they said there was a nip in the air. Clothes seem to be such a bother. Thank goodness for my nicely patterned fur. It managed to keep me cool in the warm weather and warm in the cool. However, with the nip in the air, the time in the backyard had become shorter.

The woman started talking about me possibly going into the house. Of course, this was all part of my master plan. I was just about ready to start packing when I heard her say I had to be checked out by the vet first. I really wasn't sure what a vet was, but I knew I didn't like the sound of it.

My man came into the garage and started talking to me in the way only he could. He was petting me and talking softly, and I fell for it. Next thing I knew, I was in a large carrier and on the move. It was like déjà vu all over again. My heart sank as I was placed in his car. I thought they liked me, and now I was being sent away, again.

After a short drive, the car stopped. I was carefully lifted out of the car, and we went into a building. I thought I recognized the smell, but I couldn't remember from where. I was hunkered down in the cage, defeated.

We sat in a big room for a short time with other animals of various types. I assumed this was some sort of disintegration chamber where we would all be liquidated. (I have a very vivid imagination.) The carrier was lifted, and we slowly walked to a smaller room. The door to my carrier was opened on a table, and I was asked to come out. I THINK NOT! A hand reached in and grabbed hold of me to drag me out. As I came out of the carrier, I saw my man there. I also saw a stranger, a female. She was not bad looking either, for a human. The demeanor of the humans was not that of death and destruction, but of calm and kindness. I began to relax, a little.

I soon remembered where I had smelled the smell before. It was the doctor's office that began the upheaval in my life. She was different, though. Gentle, but all business. They were inspecting my coat, looking for fleas. Fleas! On me? Impossible. She placed a very cold thing on my belly and started poking around in places polite cats don't talk about. She then put something in my butt, and I immediately let them know I wasn't happy. It took both of them to hold it and me in place. After about an hour, (remember I don't own a watch) she pulled it out. It might not have been that long to them, but it was my butt!

They were talking about what a nice cat I was and that I would make a nice housecat. I did not really grasp the whole concept of housecat at the time, but I would. The female then picked me up and was headed toward another door. I was afraid this was the end, but I noticed my man sit on a chair to wait for me.

In this new place, there were several more people rushing around. I was placed on yet another very cold table with a very strange smell. They took my paw and began rubbing a strange liquid on it. Then I saw this shiny, long, thin object coming toward my paw. The humans were talking very softly to me, and I was totally relaxed when all of a sudden, I felt this excruciating pain in my paw. I tried to get away, but they had a firm grip on me. Then, as fast as the pain came, it stopped, sort of. They wiped my paw again and then picked me up.

I was concerned about moving again until I saw my man standing up and opening the carrier door. He told me I was a good boy, and we would be going home soon. My heart skipped a beat. Home. It had a nice ring to it. We went back to the larger room we started in and sat down again. My man continued to talk to me, but left me in the carrier. I guess he didn't want somebody else thinking I was so cute they would want me.

We were called back into the little room and sat down. The female was talking to my man, and it sounded very serious. I heard my man say he would have to think about it and talk to his wife. He sounded different somehow, upset. He picked up the carrier with me still in it, and we went back to the car. Instead of starting the engine, he began talking into this little box. He was now very upset, crying. He finished talking and started the car.

He talked to me during the ride home, but it wasn't the same. He sounded different, but I listened anyway. I was very worried about his tone—and my future. He kept telling me everything was going to work out, but I wasn't sure whom he was trying to convince.

We arrived back at the house, and he released me from my carrier. I was stretching and getting ready for a little roughhousing, but he went directly into the house. I quickly moved close to the door so I could hear what was going on. (Cats have exceptional hearing, you know.) My man was very upset, and he was saying things like, "put down" and "isolation." My woman was very calm and saying things like "wait and see" and "second opinion." I was confused and nervous.

A short time later, my man came out and we went for a walk. Neither of us had our usual bounce in our step. We just seemed to be going through the motions. It was a short walk, too. We got back home and he said goodnight. I curled up in my box and tried to sleep. I needed to sleep on everything that had happened.

The next day, after my man arrived home, I was again placed in the carrier and taken off on another adventure. We stopped, but he said nothing. We walked into another strange place, but it, too, had a familiar smell. I was now becoming all too familiar with this smell. After a short wait, we went into a small room where I was asked to come out of the carrier. My man reached into the carrier and pulled me out. I was a little surprised, but gave in and got out of the carrier.

Another female started to stroke me and talk calmly to me. She and my man were talking about my painful experience yesterday. She weighed me and said I was all muscle. I work out and watch what I eat, so I was pleased she noticed. After another cold thing on my belly and the humiliation of something else put up my butt, I was carried into yet another room. She took my paw and wiped it with that strange smelling liquid from yesterday. I saw that same long, shiny thing that caused so much pain yesterday headed toward my paw, and I froze. I thought if I gave them a little growl, they would stop, but she only continued to talk softly. She jammed that thing in my paw, and there was that sharp, intense pain again. I later learned that thing was called a needle.

She carried me back to my man and said to wait for a few minutes. He held me close, and I licked my paw. I didn't like the taste of that liquid, but I did like him holding me. I was in pain and once again humiliated, so I refused to purr, but I did lie in his lap.

The soft talking female returned and said she confirmed the diagnosis. They talked about something called FIV, and she said there were many schools of thought. Unless the cats fought and drew blood, there was nothing to worry about. He thanked her and put me back in my carrier. We got in the car and went home.

My woman met him in the driveway, and he said it was confirmed; I had Feline AIDS. I had no idea what that all meant, but it seemed to be upsetting to them. He put the carrier down, and I happily got out. He picked me up and held me close, and she was petting me and talking softly. It was an odd sensation because they were being very affectionate, but sounding very upset. I didn't know exactly what was going on, but I figured I could use it to my advantage.

# Entering the House

Instead of leaving me in the garage, I was carried into the house. This is what I had been hoping for, and now it was a dream come true. I walked around cautiously, but with confidence, tail held high. I explored the couch and the fireplace. I also walked toward this very large thing that looked like a piece of broccoli covered with carpeting, but smelled like the girls. I was following my man into the kitchen, the living room, and the dining room. This was all pretty standard stuff because my last house had this stuff, too, except the broccoli.

What happened next was a whole new experience for me; I was allowed to go upstairs. I ran up those stairs and began to explore every nook and cranny. My man picked me up and carried me to what turned out to be the bathroom for the whole family. He pointed out the litter box and, of course, I had to check it out. Since I was accustomed to using the great outdoors; this sand stuff felt a little strange, but I knew I would adjust.

In a room called a bedroom, I was called up onto a soft cushy thing called a bed. This was unlike anything I had ever felt before. My heart was pounding like a new baby kitten, but I was acting very cool. As I sniffed a little around the bed, I smelled the girls. They were not on the bed at the time, but they had been, and I would get to see them.

We explored the remainder of the house, paying particular attention to anything soft I could lie on. Back in the family room, my humans put down some bowls with crunchy food and water and something else, moist stuff. I sniffed it cautiously and decided it smelled pretty good. I took a small taste and it was incredible.

I gobbled the entire portion and went looking for more. I found the girls and must say their reaction was a little rude. I walked over to them to say hi and see if they had the same delicious food I had just finished. The tan and white babe puffed her tail and growled at me. The gray one hit me—hit me! It's not like I took their food from them. My woman did not like me around their food either and shoved me away saying I had my own food. I stomped back to my dishes and had some "crunchies."

When I was full, I went and sat in front of the fireplace to clean up. It was very warm and comfortable, and I found myself getting drowsy. I found a nice spot on the rug and curled up in a ball. I was very content now and felt safer than I ever had before. I was happy and felt wanted. This was my family and I was home.

# Settling In

I woke up some time later with no idea how long I had slept. I knew it had been a while, and I felt a strange twinge in my stomach. I thought it was just excitement, but I was wrong—I was hungry. I got up slowly, stretched, and walked over to the bowls sitting by the big glass doors. To my surprise, there was still water and that really good crunchy stuff in them. I couldn't believe my luck; there was food available all the time! I had some crunchies and washed them down with a little water. After refueling, I decided to use the "facilities" before again searching for the girls.

I thought maybe they might not have noticed I had moved in, but I soon found out they were just trying to ignore the fact. I knew in my heart they had adjusted and were ready to become friends. Once again, I was way off base. I looked all around downstairs, but there was no sign of them, so I decided to venture upstairs and look for them.

I walked up the stairs slowly; surely they were only hiding and waiting to play with me. When I got to the top step, I expected to see them jump out and smile in a kitty way, but they were not there. Figuring I would play along, I walked from room to room in search of them. I was also checking out all the places to sleep up there and thought I should start marking my territory. I finally got to the last room, which appeared to have the biggest place to sleep and jumped up on the bed. To my wondering eyes, there they were, both of them, sleeping.

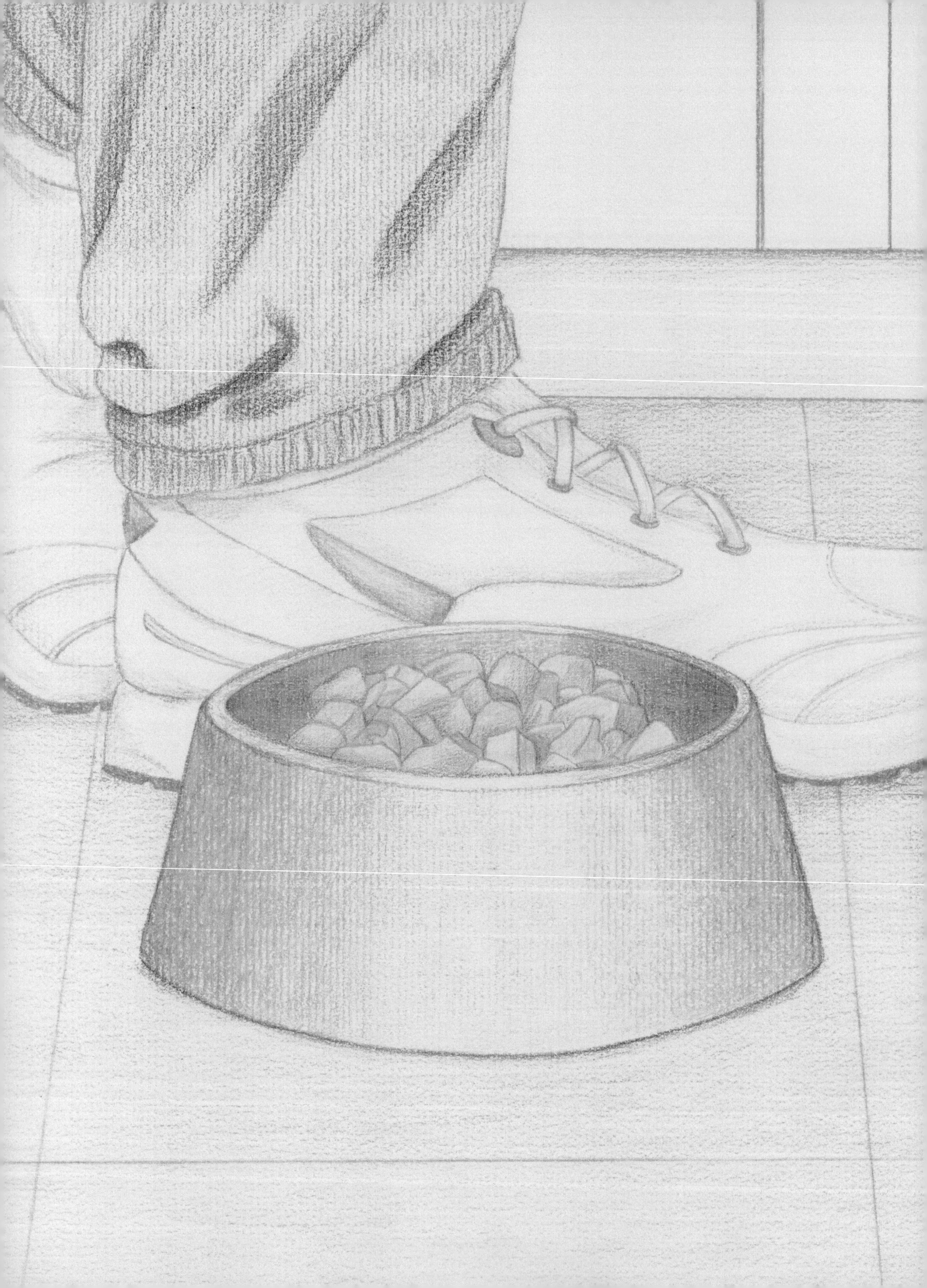

I figured they would want me to get close and lie down with them. Once again, I was very wrong. The gray babe reached back and swatted me with a right hook, and the little orange fireball jumped down and walked away. Just as I was recovering from the first blow, I got smacked again with a left jab. I decided retreat was my only option and jumped off the bed. I figured they were just playing hard to get. I had no idea at the time just how hard to get they meant to be.

It was becoming painfully obvious that I needed to come up with a new way to become friends. I slithered to another room that had a bed and jumped up on it to think. I curled up in a thinking position and began racking my brain for a new plan. I guess I curled up too well, because I fell asleep. Once again, I had no idea how long I had been asleep, but my woman was stroking my coat and talking to me. I was still a little foggy from my nap, so I am not sure what she was saying, but it felt good to be stroked again in a kind way. I really tried to hold off on showing how happy I was to be here, but to no avail—I began to purr, softly at first, but soon a deep, affectionate purr. She seemed to really like it, too.

All of this was keeping me from my mission of becoming friends with my new housemates. Suddenly, I heard a strange noise in the kitchen and thought it warranted investigation. Apparently, this was a good thing because both girls were hanging around the human male, and the little orange one was yowling. Wow, something smelled good. I was asked to follow my man, and he placed another bowl on the floor for me

I walked over and sniffed, not wanting to appear too anxious, but decided to dig in and eat. I could not believe my luck. I was not only in a nice house with lots of different places to sleep, but I was going to have lots of food and two caring humans. I knew I was going to really, really like it here.

After I tasted my food, I went to where the girls had been eating to see if they had anything different. It smelled the same as what I had, but just to be sure, I checked out their bowls anyway. This seemed to upset the woman because she pushed me away from the bowls. I was confused, but, of course, complied. Since I had eaten a nice meal, it was now time for a nap; I am, after all, a cat. I thought I would check out the large broccoli thing that sat next to my food. I wasn't really sure what it was, but I knew it was a great place to sharpen my claws. I jumped up to the top level, and to my surprise, there was one of my little friends. I was just about to start sniffing when I got smacked on the side of the head. Once again the woman intervened and snatched me off the thing. Once again, I was confused.

I guess the couch would be a good place to rest for now, but I would have to try that big thing again sometime soon. I jumped on the couch and ran right into my gray buddy. Excited, I took a couple of steps toward her, and smack! I got it right in the head. What is it with these two? Unlike the orange cat, this one did not move and was ready to hit me again, so I scooted to the far end of the couch. This making friends thing was not going to be easy. I curled up and began to think yet again, but, you guessed it, I fell asleep.

# Taking a Break

Once again, I woke up feeling a little groggy but decided a little snack would help. I stretched, jumped down from the couch, and wandered over to my food bowl. Boy that sounded good, my food bowl. It had been a long time since I had something to call my own, and now it seemed I had the "dog by the tail," so to speak.

My bowl was almost empty, so I went to check out the bowls in the kitchen. I still didn't understand why there were so many bowls with all the same thing, but food was food. I managed a few gulps before the woman came in and caught me. She didn't really yell, but told me to eat my own food. As we walked into the area where my bowl was, she realized it was empty. I sat and looked pitiful as I gazed into the empty bowl and then at her. She melted, told me to hold on, and went to the cupboard where the food was kept. I had an urge to save her some steps and go eat right there on the counter, but I decided it was better to act a little bored. I began to lick my paw and paid no attention to the bowl being fixed (or so she thought). Finally, after what seemed like an eternity, she walked in and placed the bowl on the floor next to me. I looked at it and walked away, not far, mind you, just to the water bowl. After all, I was going to be changing courses and needed to cleanse my pallet.

The woman looked frustrated and said something, but I don't know what. She walked away, and as soon as she was out of sight, I lunged at the bowl. This new stuff was great and I really liked it.

After eating my fill, I, of course, washed up. The sun was shining in the window, and I decided I needed to sit and think about my situation. I was thrilled with my new digs, and of course the human male was the best. The females of the house, however, were another matter—all of them. I used to have quite a reputation with the ladies, but I couldn't make any leeway with any of them. I needed a new strategy, but what?

As luck would have it, my man came and opened the door. It was time to go out and play. I loved playing with him, and he seemed to enjoy it as well. We chased each other around the yard, and I climbed part way up a tree. Just as I got comfortable in the tree, the women of the house came out. Of course the furry ones ignored me, but the human woman yelled at my man to get me out of the tree. We both ignored her and continued to play. This seemed to work for him because she went and sat down and left us alone. That's it! I would ignore the girls.

It would come to a point when they could no longer stand it, and they would come around. Finally, I knew what to do. It was brilliant, and I had thought of it all by myself.

My plan was working wonderfully. I was not paying any attention to the girls, and, oddly enough, the human woman had not yelled at me since the inception of my plan. Every time one of the girls got close to me, I just flicked my tail and walked away. I wouldn't even look to see if she was following. This went on for days, and I knew it had to be tearing them apart. How could they stand being away from me for so long?

After about a week, I decided they had suffered long enough and I would end this standoff. I had to decide how to approach them again and tell them all was forgiven. I also had to pick just the right time. I needed to think, so I curled up on the couch. Unfortunately, I had to get comfortable to think, and, well, you guessed it; I fell asleep. Only the Top Cat himself knows how long I had been asleep, but I felt refreshed and ready to end my standoff.

I looked all over the house for the girls and found them curled up with the woman. Discretion being the better part of valor, I decided to wait a little longer to grace them with my company. Tomorrow was another day, and I wasn't going anywhere.

# Halloween

Halloween, as I later heard it called, started out as any other day. We ate breakfast, got brushed, used the box, and after the humans left, went back to bed. Just another day like any other, or so I thought.

First to arrive home was "Mama," as she was now dubbed. She was rushing around getting things ready for dinner in a faster way than usual. I was excited because this usually meant a really big meal with lots of tasty leftovers. I was trying to remain casual, but my mind was working overtime. Since arriving at this house, I had not had a bad meal. I didn't have to hunt for it, and I was always open to trying new things.

"Daddy" arrived home, and it was time for us to eat. He placed our dishes in our usual places, and we all gobbled down dinner. I was gently cleaning up and wondering when the "real meal of human food" was coming when I noticed both humans standing at the counter, eating what looked like sandwiches. This made no sense, so I continued to observe from a distance.

The entire routine of our evening was being disrupted. Normally, we spent the evening in the big room with the fireplace, and most of the lights in the front of the house were off. This evening was different. The porch light was on, and a small table had been placed by the door. I was just about to jump up and see what was in the bowl on the table when I heard Mama yell. Knowing I was busted, I walked away.

Just as I was getting ready to take a short nap, the doorbell rang. The girls did not like the bell and scampered up the stairs. (Unknown to me at the time, they had been through this ritual before and knew what to expect.) I, being a good host, accompanied Daddy to the front door to greet our guests. When he opened the door, there was a loud scream of, 'Trick or treat!' I like to think I would be very protective of my humans if they were ever threatened, but I was totally unprepared for this type of sneak attack. The creatures standing at the door were unlike any I had ever seen before. The hair on my back was standing up, and my tail was as full as I could make it. I was ready to defend them with my life when I heard Mama laughing. She was looking at the creatures at the door and talking to them. Daddy had grabbed the bowl off the small table and thrust it at the creatures. Obviously, this was a payoff to keep from being harmed. After dropping things from the bowl into the bags they were carrying, the creatures turned and walked away, satisfied with the payoff. I was truly relieved, but very much on the alert, determined that no harm would ever come to my humans.

A very short time later, the bell rang again, and yet another group of creatures stood at the door. A human accompanied this group. I figured he had refused to pay and had been taken captive. He was being paraded around to show others what would happen if they, too, chose to be so foolish. Again, my humans paid the bounty. The thing that confused me the most was, why did they keep opening the door? These creatures were, by comparison, very small and clearly no match for us, but they kept paying. This odd behavior continued for some time.

I was getting concerned because the bowl containing the payments was getting low. What would happen if the bowl emptied and they kept coming? Would I become the man of the house, all alone to take care of the girls? Worse yet, would I lose my house?

Just as I was getting myself all worked up, the front light was turned off, and we moved back into the family room to watch TV. It was over and we had survived. I might never know what really happened that night, but I hoped it would never happen again.

# The Mistake

The weather was turning colder, and our time outside was getting shorter. We still went out and played on what they called the weekend, but time during the week was limited because it was dark so early. Apparently humans can't see in the dark as well as we cats. (And they call themselves superior beings!) I couldn't even go out on the indoor porch to lie in the sun because Mama kept telling me it was too cold. Did she forget I lived outside for a period of time? Granted, I didn't like it, but I did it.

I wandered out to the garage one afternoon when my humans were bringing in groceries to have a look around my old stomping grounds. Since they didn't realize I was out there, the door was closed and I was left out. I checked and found out that the "doggie door" was still working and walked outside. I figured as long as I was out, I should go and visit some of my old friends from the neighborhood.

It was sunny so I knew I had plenty of time before anyone missed me. I ran down the block and began looking for my pals. I hadn't gotten too far when I spied a new addition to the block. She was a beautiful—white, long hair, with gorgeous green eyes. She flashed me a smile, and I knew I had to stop and get to know this beauty. We began talking, and she told me she just moved in with a nice family. I was explaining the ropes to her of how to wrap her humans around her tail, when she started telling me about something strange that happened a few nights ago. It was about the aliens walking around collecting bounty. She informed me she was frightened and had hidden under her family's bed. I told her I stayed with my family and was ready to fight to the death to save them. She told me I was very brave.

We continued to talk for a long time, when it started to get dark. I looked up to the sky and noticed it was getting very gray, and the wind had really begun to howl. Since my family had no idea I was out, I figured I should say so long for now and head home. I told my new friend, Lulu to get inside where it was safe, and I turned to walk home.

I ran back through the same yards I had crossed earlier. It was getting scary because the wind was blowing so hard, things were flying around the yards. I narrowly missed getting hit by a trash can lid when it started to rain. It was coming down hard and fast, and I considered ducking under a porch to wait it out. I thought about my nice warm house and my family and decided to keep going.

Holes in the yards were beginning to fill with water, and I was getting soaked. I was getting close to home when a loud booming noise scared me. I was slowly recovering when I saw a bright flash of light. All of a sudden, the entire neighborhood went black, and I froze. I wanted to run home but was momentarily confused about which way to go. I stopped, took a deep breath, and figured out which way to run. Within minutes, I saw my house and, after checking both ways for cars, ran up the driveway. I pushed open the "doggie door," and knew I was OK, wet but safe.

After shaking to get off some of the water, I began scratching at the door. I was getting cold and stepped up my effort to get back inside. Finally, after what seemed like hours, the door opened, and there stood Mama. She was surprised to see me; after all, I did not look my best. I gave her my most pathetic look and scampered into the house. She yelled for Daddy to get some towels to dry me off, but I didn't want to be roughed up with towels. I ran through the house toward the stairs so I could go up on the bed and rest after my experience. To my surprise, Mama took off after me and tried to grab me. Under normal circumstances, I love to be chased, but I was cold, wet, and tired and just wanted to lie down. I was just about to jump onto the bed when Daddy grabbed me, wrapped me in a towel, and took me to the bathtub. He began rubbing and really messing up my beautiful coat.

For several hours, (actually probably only minutes) I was rubbed dry. I was also brushed within an inch of my life. The girls sat on the sink and watched the whole humiliating affair with big grins on their faces. My humans were very quiet through all this, and I just wanted to forget the whole thing, when all of a sudden Mama asked me if I was crazy, sneaking out like that.

She picked me up and began talking softly and telling me how much they would miss me if I were gone. She was petting me and making me purr really loud. I wanted to show her how much I appreciated her kindness, so I gave her a little nip on the chin. Boy, did she turn on a dime. I just don't understand. All the other girls I've ever given a little nip really liked it. Humans are very confusing sometimes. Needless to say, we never spoke of that moment again.

I was sure things were getting back to normal after our excitement of the last few weeks. I stayed in the house, and we had no more visitors, for which I was truly thankful. I liked my happy routine and didn't like change anymore. Little did I know what kind of thrilling things were yet to come.

# First Taste of Turkey

One day after breakfast, my humans started talking about something called "holidays." Mama said she needed to make a list so we could have a full Thanksgiving dinner with turkey and everything. Daddy seemed very excited about the prospect of this and told me I would really like the taste of turkey. Up to this point I enjoyed everything I had eaten, but I was certainly open to new things.

I tried, as usual, to watch the happenings around the house casually. I did not want anyone to think I was becoming excited about this holiday thing, especially since the girls seemed to care less. It was, however, becoming more and more difficult. Strange decorations began to appear around the house. I was very interested in checking things out and several times was caught sniffing them up on the tables. I became confused, again. If I bothered the girls, I was in trouble, but if I left them alone and explored other things, I was in trouble.

One weekend, a lot of bags were brought into the house. Of course, as a cat, I liked all types of bags, but these were filled to the brim. I had learned long before that when bags like this came into the house, we all sat and watched carefully because our food cans usually came out of them. There was a lot more stuff coming out of these particular bags, though. The counters were full and I was going to inspect, but just as I was ready to jump, I heard Mama tell me to not even think about it. I swear I saw the girls smile at me, once again getting in trouble. I wanted to tell them off, but outnumbered as usual, so I left.

A few days later, while Mama and Daddy were finishing their breakfast, we all went and sat on the couch. I jumped on Daddy's lap, and with the girls sitting with Mama, we started watching something called a parade on the TV. It was all pretty boring, but my humans seemed to be enjoying it. I was just dozing off when Mama said something about Santa Claus, the end of the parade, and time to start the turkey. What is a Santa Claus? Daddy didn't seem too interested, so I stayed with him and went back to sleep.

I woke up by myself on the couch. I jumped down, stretched, and without thinking, headed for my food dish. Just as I was about to have a snack, I got a sniff of something wonderful. I walked into the kitchen and saw the girls sitting very attentively in front of the oven. They never even looked in my direction when I sat down next to them. There were some wonderful smells surrounding us, and I couldn't wait to find out what was going on.

Mama came in and chased us out of the way so she could get near the oven. Daddy started putting things from pots in bowls and carrying them into the dining room. I knew this had to be something special because we didn't use this table very often. The girls were getting very excited, and I knew it wouldn't be long now. Mama opened the oven, and the most wonderful smell came rushing into the kitchen. She leaned in and pulled out a pan containing some brown thing. Daddy came in and put the thing on the counter and began sharpening a knife. It smelled so good, I didn't know why we were wasting time with a knife, let's all just dig in!

He cut up the brown thing and put it on a big plate. Next he grabbed some of the plates reserved for us when we get a special treat. The girls were dancing around his legs, and I have to admit, I was a little jealous; he was, after all, my man. Oh well, we all went into the dining room, and Mama placed plates down with some of this stuff called turkey.

The girls started to eat quickly, but I thought I would play it cool, so I acted a little bored and walked to the plate slowly to have a little sniff. I had never smelled anything like this before and realized I needed to give it a little taste. It was wonderful and before I knew it, I had finished every bite. I began to wash up, thinking that was all there was, but I noticed the girls still sitting there, staring up at the table. It worked; more of this wonderful treat was placed on all our plates. We gobbled it down, and after cleaning up, went to find a nice place to sleep, soon to be joined by our humans. I'm still not sure what this holiday called Thanksgiving is all about, but I know I really, really like it.

# First Christmas

With the excitement of Thanksgiving behind us, I thought life would settle down. Little did I know, we were just beginning the hustle and bustle known as the Christmas season. Life was going to be far from calm.

I noticed Mama bringing lots of packages into the house. Even on ordinary days, the girls and I usually watch with great anticipation because there is usually food for us in at least one bag. Unlike those other times though, there was no food. More decorations were being put all over the house. I tried to inspect as many of them as I could, but many were out of my reach. I learned a while back not to leap on any counters or shelves (when my humans were home anyway). It takes a lot of restraint on my part, but I really like my happy home and do not want to do anything to ruin it.

I was busy watching Mama bring more bags in the house when Daddy came in carrying a tree. I, of course, thought the tree was for me since I could no longer go out and play. I knew he enjoyed our time outside as much as I did, but I never figured he would get me a tree.

He set it up in the living room, which was odd, since we hardly ever used that room. I assumed it was because there was less furniture and more room to run and play. It was carefully placed in a big stand, which was then filled with water. Not only did I have a tree to play in, I no longer had to go to the other room to get a drink. Did I have the best family, or what? As soon as he finished, I walked over and took a little drink. The water was different somehow, sweet. I appreciated the gesture, but I would stick to my other water dish.

I carefully walked around the tree, looking for a good place to start my climb. I found a spot and jumped. This was not like my tree outside; it was sticky, and something was poking me all over. I was looking for a branch to sit on when Mama came in and yelled for me to get out of the tree. I was very anxious to comply, but every which way I turned, I got poked some more. I decided I needed to get out of this tree and took a deep breath, but before I could jump out, the tree began to sway back and forth, and I was going down.

The tree crashed to the floor with a loud thud, and I ran for my life. The big, sweet, water dish was on its side, and water was running all over the floor

Mama ran for a mop and was calling for Daddy to come help her clean up. He saw the tree on its side and asked what happened. I did not want to be anywhere near that tree and sat at the top of the steps, licking the sticky stuff off my paws.

Mama was explaining that I had tried to climb the tree, and it fell over. Daddy found this very funny which, needless to say, made the situation even worse. She told him it was his job to teach me to stay out of the tree. After my climb, getting poked, sticky, and then falling over, I had no intention of ever getting back in that tree. I went to my bed, finished cleaning up, and tried to calm down.

After a nice, restful sleep, I went back downstairs and found the girls walking gently under the tree. They were rubbing their backs on things dangling from the branches. I wanted to warn them of the dangers involved, but when they saw me, they just walked away. Along with a lot of dangly things, there were also lights on the tree. I didn't care how appealing they tried to make it, I wasn't getting near it again.

A few days later, boxes and other types of packages were placed under the tree. I had never seen anything like this before and had no idea what was going on. The packages had pretty paper, and some even had bows on them. I noticed OJ, the tan and white babe, liked to take bows and run around with them. She seemed to really being enjoying herself, so I thought I would try one. I chewed on it and tossed it like she was doing, but I have to admit, I did not see the appeal. Give me a good shoelace anytime.

One day called Christmas, we all got up, had breakfast, and went to sit by the tree. The lights were turned on, even though it was daytime, and packages were passed back and forth. OJ got a little package with a bow and started to rip the paper. Missi, my gray buddy, also got a package, but she did not tear into it like OJ. She waited patiently for Mama to start to open it for her. I never had anything like this before and wasn't sure what was going on. All of a sudden, there were several packages placed in front of me. Gifts for me! I was overwhelmed. I sniffed cautiously and began pawing at the first package. I pounced on it and ripped the paper. It was great fun, but what was inside was even better, my own sock filled with catnip. We were all opening gifts and playing. I never before had so much fun.

A short time later, we had another great turkey meal and relaxed in front of the fire. I now had lots of new toys to play with and some great new tasty treats to snack on. I still don't know what this Christmas is all about, but I know I like it a lot.

# New Year's Eve

The day started out like any other. Our humans went to work and we slept. They came home, we ate, they watched TV, and we slept. It was good to have our lives back to normal.

The doorbell rang, which caused Missi and OJ to run up the stairs. I, however, was curious to see who was calling at this late hour. I heard the familiar voice of our neighbor, but also some strange voices. We were all very comfortable, and I personally didn't think we needed company, but nevertheless, they were invited in. To make matters worse, they came and sat on my couch.

Daddy was talking with the group while Mama was busy in the kitchen fixing some food. This immediately made me soften my position on the company. Before long, there was a tray of different cheeses, some kind of beef thing, crackers, and veggies. The cheese had my interest, but the rest... Finally, there was a tray brought in, and it contained, oh, could it be? Shrimp! I'd had shrimp once and longed for the day when I could taste it again.

The humans all ate and talked happily while I tried to figure out my strategy. I walked around the table a few times to find my best vantage point for grabbing a few tasty morsels. They all had the table pretty well blocked, but I knew there had to be a way. Just as I was about to step back for a better look, Daddy reached down and gave me some shrimp. I thought I had died and gone to kitty heaven. I sat right next to him and was supplied with cheese, beef stick, and of course, shrimp. The girls had no idea what they were missing.

We all continued to visit, and of course I was being very cute, so everyone was paying close attention to me. There was lots of petting, rubbing, and cooing at me, and naturally, I enjoyed every minute. I was getting a little sleepy and decided I had had enough to eat, so it was time for a short nap. I curled up on top of the carpeted broccoli, closed my eyes, and dropped of to sleep.

I was having wonderful dreams of running through a meadow after a nice rabbit when all of a sudden, people were screaming. I woke with a start and had my claws at the ready. I thought my family was being attacked. They were ringing bells and blowing into something that made a horrible noise. I figured the strangers had attacked, when all of a sudden, they all started kissing and hugging each other. First Mama and Daddy gave each other a big hug and kiss. Then they hugged and kissed the neighbor, the strangers, and finally, me. Everyone came over to me and gave me a great big kiss and scratched me on top of my head. I still had my claws ready, but enjoyed the attention.

They poured some kind of liquid into glasses, and I heard the glasses clink together. I went over to Daddy to smell the liquid and did not like it, so I walked away.

They ate some more, visited for a short time, said "Happy New Year" a lot to each other, and then, as quickly as the festivities had begun, they were over.

My humans cleaned up the kitchen and, of course, gave me a little more shrimp. We all climbed the stairs and headed for bed. The girls moved a little, giving Mama some room, and I curled up next to Daddy. I was trying to decipher everything that had happened over the last few hours. These humans have some strange activities, but I know in time, I will come to understand all of them.

# The Good Life

Well, all in all, it has been a great year. I admit it didn't start off too good, but it sure ended with a bang (no pun intended). I found a great family, a nice house, lots of food to call my own, and built-in roommates. Life certainly is good.

I hope we never encounter the small alien creatures again, but I do like the turkey associated with Thanksgiving and the presents that came with Christmas. I didn't really like the horns and bells of New Year's, but the shrimp—yum!

Yes, life with my new family is really good. I fell in the proverbial stinky litter box and came out smelling like catnip. With all the exciting events of this past year, I know the future will probably be a little boring, but sometimes boring is good. Whatever the future holds, I know I can handle it now with this loving family. I will be ready for any and all new exciting adventures that may lie ahead.